EUPHONIA AND THE FLOOD

By Mary Calhoun

Pictures By Simms Taback

Parents' Magazine Press/New York

Text copyright © 1976 by Mary Calhoun
Illustrations copyright © 1976 by Simms Taback
All rights reserved
Printed in the United States of America

Library of Congress Cataloging in Publication Data

Calhoun, Mary.
  Euphonia and the flood.

  SUMMARY: Curious to see where the flood is going,
an old woman packs her broom and pig into her boat
and sets out to follow it.
  [1. Floods—Fiction] I. Taback, Simms. II. Title.
PZ7.C1278Eu [E] 75-19274
ISBN 0-8193-0836-6   ISBN 0-8193-0837-4 lib. bdg.

To Rita, in memory of Aunt Minnie

One time there was an old woman named Euphonia who had a broom, a pig and a boat. The broom's name was Briskly, the pig's name was Fatly, and the boat's name was Mary Anne.

Euphonia always said, "If a thing is worth doing, it's worth doing well."

So the broom swept briskly, the pig lived fatly, and the boat floated very nicely, thank you. As for Euphonia, she did well by every living soul who came up her doorpath.

But one time a flood came up her doorpath, all kinds of water sashaying out of the creek banks. Water, it whipped and swashled around until it came right through Euphonia's front door.

"For a flood," she said, "that creek is doing right well. But we can't just sit here hollering for help. We'll go and see where all this floodwater is a-rushing to."

So the old woman packed Briskly and Fatly into Mary Anne, untied
the boat and pushed off down the creek.
"Row, Fatly," said Euphonia.

The pig took the oars and he rowed fatly. Euphonia took the broom and she swept the floodwaters briskly, keeping the tree-boughs and trash from bumping into the boat. Mary Anne, she floated very nicely, thank you.

And they all streamed down the creek, neat as needles,
without snagging up on anything. Euphonia smiled and said,
"If a thing is worth doing, it's worth doing well."

But before long, she saw a skunk scramble onto a tiny island
and just sit there, sopping wet.
"Safe at last!" cried the skunk.

"Safe, nothing!" said Euphonia. "Creek's on the rise. And what are you going to eat, sitting there on that mud hump, maybe for days? Better pile in with us."

The old woman caught onto the mud hump with Briskly and held the boat there.

"I'm better off than I was," insisted the skunk, patting the mud with his paws and staying put.

"Silly skunk!" exclaimed Euphonia. "You'll either starve or drown. Lean over, Fatly."

The pig leaned over fatly, and Euphonia swept the skunk briskly across the pig's back onto the boat. Mary Anne, she floated very nicely, thank you.

"There!" said Euphonia. "If a thing is worth doing, it's worth doing well."

The skunk shook himself good, so they all got wet,

and the boatload of them popped on down the creek flood.

Pretty soon the old woman saw three chickens squatting on a piece of henhouse roof. Roof was floating in a backwater of the flood.

"You can't go nor come, puddling around back there," called Euphonia. But the chickens clucked, "We're better off than we were."

"Shiftless chickens!" exclaimed Euphonia. "If you're gonna be in a flood, you might as well see the flood, where it's a-going. Why, you could even row that henhouse roof with your wings.

Pull over there, Fatly."

So the pig pulled over there fatly and, with the broom, the old woman hitched Mary Anne's rope briskly to the henhouse roof. Then they all scooted on down the creek, boatload of them with the three chickens in tow.

The chickens, they fluttered and squawked about their fast ride on the flood, but Euphonia only smiled.

"There! If a thing is worth doing, it's worth doing well."

By and by, they came to a bear. Old bear, he was thrashing around in the flood, clinging to a tree branch and shouting, "Help! Help!" But when he saw all that shebang a-swarming down the creek at him— boat, pig, skunk, old woman and broom, plus a henhouse roof full of chickens— the bear cried, "Keep away!"

Euphonia called back, "We're your help. Climb right on in with us."

But the bear paddled up a great splash, crying, "I'm better off alone! Tree branch, it'll save me."

"Blithery bear!" exclaimed Euphonia. "A boat is better than a branch. Catch up, Fatly."

So the pig caught up fatly, and the old woman broomed the bear and his tree branch briskly into the boat. Old bear, he settled his bottom in one end, and he liked that solid spot there. Mary Anne sank a little lower in the water where the bear sat, but still she floated very nicely, thank you.

"There!" Euphonia smiled and said. "If a thing is worth doing, it's worth doing well."

And they all sashayed on down the creek, boat and broom, old woman
and pig, skunk and bear a-holding onto his branch, with the chickens
on their henhouse roof squawking along behind.

Right about that time, the whole scramble of them came around a bend and found out exactly where the floodwater was a-going—to Farmer Stump's millpond. That pond, it was spread out to a fare-thee-well all over the hollow.

Bobbing on the water was every kind of animal riding out the flood—squirrels on branches, rabbits on logs, hop-toads on big leaves. And up ahead, the flood tipped over into a waterfall.

"Far enough!" Euphonia called out. "Fatly, pull for shore."
So the pig pulled fatly for shore. There on the high ground,
Farmer Stump had set up food-tables for all the folks who had
come floating down in the flood.

When she spied that, Euphonia said, "Now you see where the floodwater
was a-going? To a picnic, that's where! And we'd have missed it sure,
if we just stayed back home hollering for help. Very nicely done,
Mary Anne. Thank you."

So they all climbed ashore and stomped their feet on the good high ground. The bear ate honey and biscuits, the skunk ate apple pie,

the chickens ate cornbread, and the pig ate fatly of all of that, plus turnips, too.

As for Euphonia, she did well by every living soul that bobbed by her on the millpond. She broomed them out briskly. "Because," she said, "if a thing is worth doing, it's worth doing well!"

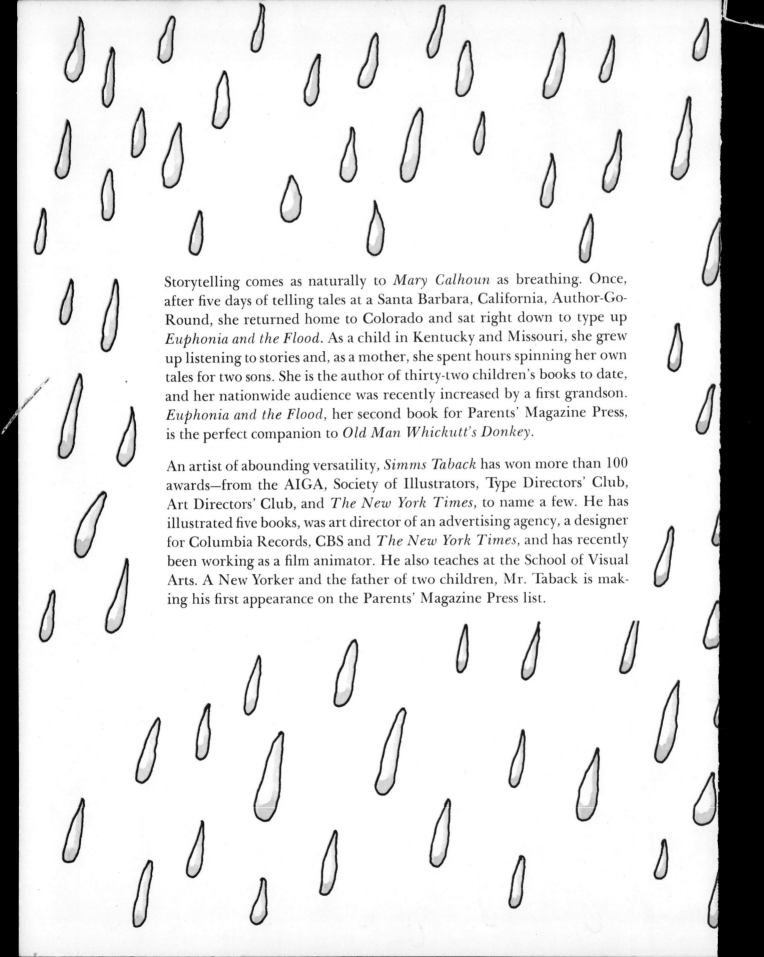

Storytelling comes as naturally to *Mary Calhoun* as breathing. Once, after five days of telling tales at a Santa Barbara, California, Author-Go-Round, she returned home to Colorado and sat right down to type up *Euphonia and the Flood*. As a child in Kentucky and Missouri, she grew up listening to stories and, as a mother, she spent hours spinning her own tales for two sons. She is the author of thirty-two children's books to date, and her nationwide audience was recently increased by a first grandson. *Euphonia and the Flood*, her second book for Parents' Magazine Press, is the perfect companion to *Old Man Whickutt's Donkey*.

An artist of abounding versatility, *Simms Taback* has won more than 100 awards—from the AIGA, Society of Illustrators, Type Directors' Club, Art Directors' Club, and *The New York Times*, to name a few. He has illustrated five books, was art director of an advertising agency, a designer for Columbia Records, CBS and *The New York Times*, and has recently been working as a film animator. He also teaches at the School of Visual Arts. A New Yorker and the father of two children, Mr. Taback is making his first appearance on the Parents' Magazine Press list.